This book belongs to:

_____

I am Born Mighty. I am Born Abel.

You've found a lucky sock!

We all have socks
but yours are lucky,
you see?

Your socks are special
they come in 3's!

Three socks are not better or worse than two, but your socks are different and they make you, you!

You have three socks where most have two.
That makes us lucky to get to love you!

XXX

You're blessed with an extra
21st chromosome

What is a chromosome?

Your body is made up of trillions of cells.
Inside of those cells are chromosomes.

Chromosomes tell your body how to grow.

They look like socks,
don't you think so?

cell

What is Down syndrome?

Down syndrome is a genetic difference. It means a person was born with an extra 21st chromosome.

That can make their growing plan a little different than other people's. But they are still "Abel" to do all the things someone else can do!

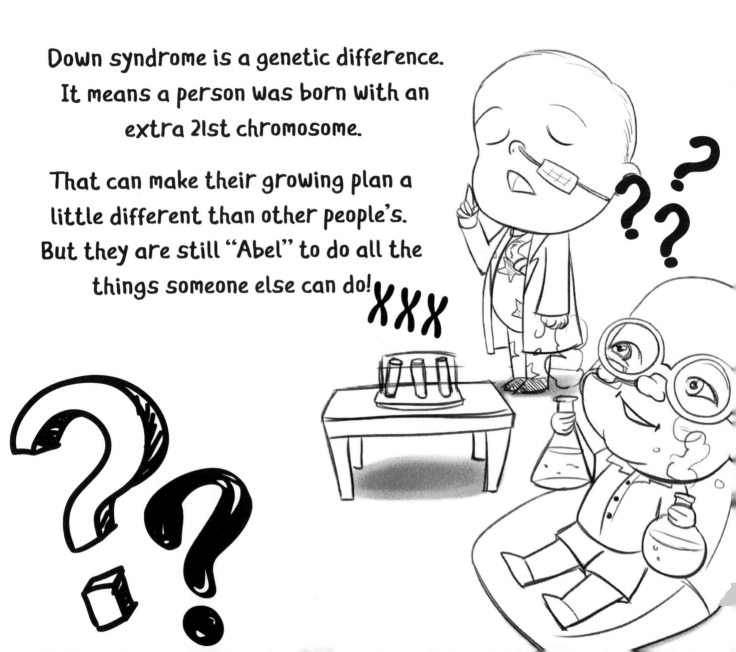

Can you spot the difference?

A chromosome is tiny indeed.

A chromosome cannot be seen.

Kids with Down syndrome
can look different too.
They may not speak quite the
same as others do.

They may take longer to learn something new,
But in many ways they are no different, it's true.

Some of us have blonde hair,
red, or brown.

Sometimes we smile.
Sometimes we frown.

We don't all have to be exactly the same to be friends with each other or play a game.

Sometimes you might hear they are always so happy, but that isn't true...

They have big feelings, we all do.

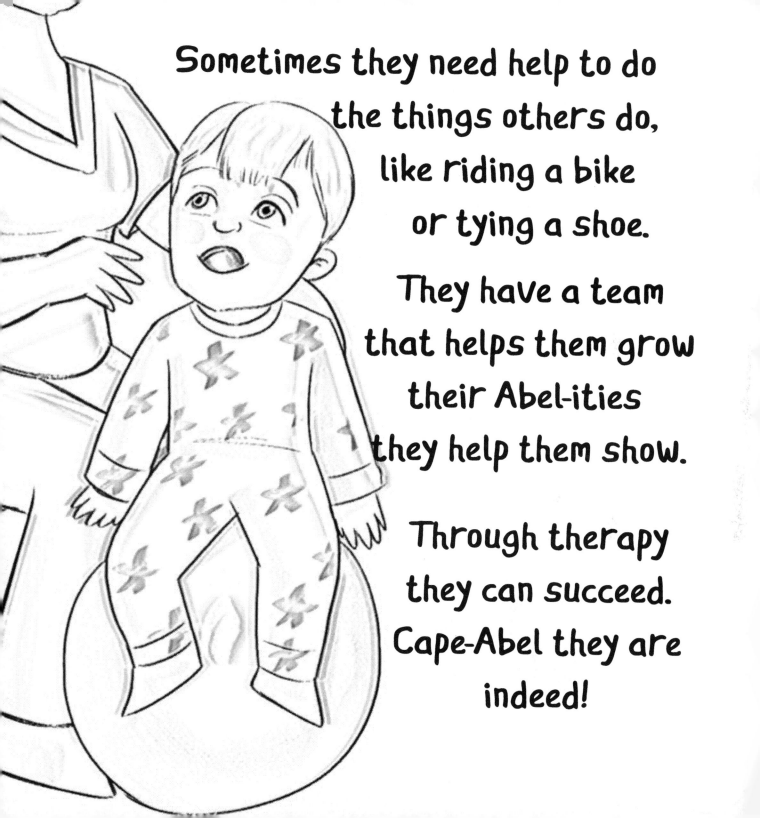

Sometimes they need help to do the things others do, like riding a bike or tying a shoe.

They have a team that helps them grow their Abel-ities they help them show.

Through therapy they can succeed. Cape-Abel they are indeed!

Sometimes kids with Down syndrome have delays, but they never let that ruin their days.

They want to laugh and play just like the others do, they say.

Do you have buddies?
What are their names?

Every shape, every size, every color and hue,
Down syndrome shines bright in all that we do.

Around the world, we do not hide,
We celebrate with joy and pride!

All unique, every face,
You, we couldn't replace.
You're lucky, you see?
Your socks come in 3s.

We're so proud of you,
The chosen few.

You have three socks where most have two.
That makes us lucky, we get to love you!

An athlete...
A baker...
An actor....
A model...
The possibilities are endless my dear child.

We wouldn't change anything if it meant changing you...
Lucky socks we are rockin' that yellow and blue.

Almond shaped eyes
we wouldn't trade for the world.

The tiniest hands
perfect to hold.

Sandal toe gaps
on your feet
oh my dear child,
they're such a treat!

We're lucky aren't we?
our socks come in 3s.

There's 3 different types of Down syndrome too!
We all still rock that yellow and blue!

There's Trisomy21, Translocation, and Mosaic,
we're different, it's ok to say it!

It's not that rare, to come in 3s
it happens in 1 of every 640 babies!

See we're lucky, lucky indeed!
full of magic is guaranteed!

Do you know anyone who is blessed with 3s?

Now when you look around, I hope that you'll see...
We're all different,
it's a great thing
to be!

Dear Parent,

Learning that your child has or will be born with Down syndrome can be quite shocking. A diagnosis delivery can leave you with a multitude of feelings. I want you to know that all of those feelings are valid and it is perfectly normal to experience a wide range of emotions following a diagnosis delivery. Your life will be different moving forward. There will be days filled with worries, sadness, and making difficult decisions. BUT, there will be so many more days that are filled with love, laughter, joy, and the celebrations of thousands of victories and milestones met.

Your child will be as much alike as they will be different from other children with Down syndrome. Your child will be as much alike as they will be different from other typically developing children. Every child is unique in their own ways and your child will be no different in that regard.

Do not expect to get all your answers from any one book or person. No one can tell you everything that your child will or will not be able to accomplish. No one can tell you all that your child will struggle with or excel at. Learn to take every day as it comes. As your child grows, you will grow with them. Savor these moments: hold, cuddle, and get to know this unique human being. Remember that this child needs what every other child needs - to be loved, accepted, and valued.

                                                    Love,

                                          Laurin & Elijah

On August 26, 2023, Abel passed away suddenly.
He stabilized briefly to say goodbye to
his family, friends, and primary nurses.

He is greatly loved and missed beyond words.

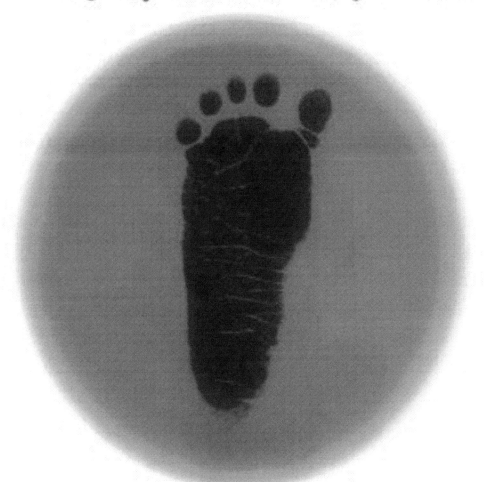

He will continue to live on through his books; inspiring hope, and
showing the worth and love of these amazing children no matter
the limitation or the duration of their beautiful lives.

Watch for the next books in the Born Abel Book Series:

This is... Trisomy 18,   Minds of All Kinds,
Oh, The Places You'll Stroll

Be sure to get your copies of Abel's first 15 books, 1st workbook, 3 Classes, 6 Coloring/Activity Books, 3 Journals & 2 Books of the Born Mighty Series: All available on Amazon.com

Remember:

All proceeds from the Born Abel Book Series go directly to the Born Abel Foundation!

Copyright © 2024 Born Abel Foundation

Published in the United States of America
All rights reserved worldwide

Authentic Endeavors Publishing / Book Endeavors
Clarks Summit PA 18411

Copyright © 2024 Illustrated by Emilian Rubio

No part of this book may be reproduced by any mechanical, photographic, or electronic process, or in the form of an audio or digital recording, nor may it be stored in any retrieval system, transmitted or otherwise, be copied for public or private use other than for fair use as brief quotation embodied in articles and review - without prior written permission of the author, illustrators or publisher.

Born Abel: More Than a Pair

Paperback ISBN: 978-1-963849-38-7

Born Abel Book Series

Made in the USA
Middletown, DE
01 August 2024